Dear Parent:
Your child's love of reading starts here!

Every child learns to read in a different way and at his or her own speed. Some go back and forth between reading levels and read favorite books again and again. Others read through each level in order. You can help your young reader improve and become more confident by encouraging his or her own interests and abilities. From books your child reads with you to the first books he or she reads alone, there are I Can Read Books for every stage of reading:

SHARED READING
Basic language, word repetition, and whimsical illustrations, ideal for sharing with your emergent reader

BEGINNING READING
Short sentences, familiar words, and simple concepts for children eager to read on their own

READING WITH HELP
Engaging stories, longer sentences, and language play for developing readers

READING ALONE
Complex plots, challenging vocabulary, and high-interest topics for the independent reader

ADVANCED READING
Short paragraphs, chapters, and exciting themes for the perfect bridge to chapter books

I Can Read Books have introduced children to the joy of reading since 1957. Featuring award-winning authors and illustrators and a fabulous cast of beloved characters, I Can Read Books set the standard for beginning readers.

A lifetime of discovery begins with the magical words "I Can Read!"

Visit www.icanread.com for information
on enriching your child's reading experience.

I Can Read!™

READING
2
WITH HELP

Good Work, Amelia Bedelia

by Peggy Parish
pictures by Lynn Sweat

HarperCollinsPublishers

Good Work, Amelia Bedelia Text copyright © 1976 by Margaret Parish Illustrations copyright © 1976, 2003 by Lynn Sweat All rights reserved. No part of this book may be used or reproduced in any manner whatsoever without written permission except in the case of brief quotations embodied in critical articles and reviews. Printed in the United States of America. For information address HarperCollins Children's Books, a division of HarperCollins Publishers, 10 East 53rd Street, New York, NY 10022. www.harpercollinschildrens.com

Library of Congress Cataloging-in-Publication Data

Parish, Peggy.
  Good work, Amelia Bedelia / by Peggy Parish ; pictures by Lynn Sweat.
    p. cm.—(An I can read book)
  "Greenwillow Books."
  Summary: Literal-minded Amelia Bedelia does household chores and gets dinner ready.
  ISBN-10: 0-688-80022-X (trade bdg.) — ISBN-13: 978-0-688-80022-2 (trade bdg.)
  ISBN-10: 0-688-84022-1 (lib. bdg.) — ISBN-13: 978-0-688-84022-8 (lib. bdg.)
  ISBN-10: 0-06-051115-X (pbk.) — ISBN-13: 978-0-06-051115-9 (pbk.)
  [1. Humorous stories.] I. Sweat, Lynn, ill. II. Title.
PZ7.P219 Goe   75-20360
[E]   CIP
                                                                                                              AC

14 15 16 17 18 LP/WOR 20   ❖

For Sam and David Rogers
with love

"Amelia Bedelia," called Mr. Rogers.

"Is the coffee ready?"

"Coming right up," said Amelia Bedelia.

She poured a cup of coffee.

She took it into the dining room.

"There," said Amelia Bedelia.

"Would you like something more?"

"Yes," said Mr. Rogers.

"Toast and an egg."

8

"Fine," said Amelia Bedelia.

She went into the kitchen.

Very quickly

Amelia Bedelia was back.

Mr. Rogers picked up the egg.

He broke it over his toast.

"Confound it, Amelia Bedelia!"

he said. "I didn't say raw egg!"

"But you didn't say to cook it,"
said Amelia Bedelia.

Mr. Rogers threw down his napkin.

"Oh, go fly a kite," he said.

Amelia Bedelia looked surprised.

"All right," she said. "If you say so."

Soon Amelia Bedelia was out in a field.

She had a kite.

"Now that was nice of Mr. Rogers,"

she said. "I do love to fly kites.

But I better get back.

Mrs. Rogers might need me."

Sure enough, Mrs. Rogers was calling,

"Amelia Bedelia."

"Here I am," said Amelia Bedelia.

"There's a lot to do,"

said Mrs. Rogers.

"Do you know how to make bread?"

"I make good corn bread,"

said Amelia Bedelia.

"No, I want white bread,"

said Mrs. Rogers.

"You are a good cook.

Just do what the recipe says."

"All right," said Amelia Bedelia.

"Here's a list of the other things
I want you to do,"
said Mrs. Rogers.
"I'll be out until dinner time."
"Don't worry," said Amelia Bedelia.
"I'll get everything done."
Mrs. Rogers left.

15

"I'll start with that bread,"
said Amelia Bedelia.
She read the recipe.
"Do tell," she said.
"I never knew
bread did magic things."

Amelia Bedelia got everything
she needed.
Quickly she mixed the dough.

Amelia Bedelia

set the pan on the table.

"Now," she said,

"you're supposed to rise.

This I've got to see."

Amelia Bedelia sat down to watch.

But nothing happened.

"Maybe you don't like to be watched.

I'll come back," said Amelia Bedelia.

"Let's see."

Amelia Bedelia got her list.

"Clean out the ashes

in the parlor fireplace.

Fill the wood box."

Amelia Bedelia went into the parlor.

She cleaned out the ashes.

And Amelia Bedelia filled

the wood box.

"That's done," said Amelia Bedelia.

"What's next?"

She read, "Pot the window-box plants.

Put the pots in the parlor."

Amelia Bedelia went outside.

She counted the plants.

Then she went into the kitchen.

"My goodness," she said.

"I need every pot for this."

So she took them all.

Amelia Bedelia potted those plants.

And she took them inside.

"Now I better tend to that bread,"

said Amelia Bedelia.

She went into the kitchen.

But the bread still sat on the table.

"Now look here," she said.

"You are supposed to rise.

Then I'm supposed to punch you down.

How can I punch if you don't rise?"

Amelia Bedelia sat down to think.

"Maybe that pan is too heavy,"

she said.

"I better help it rise."

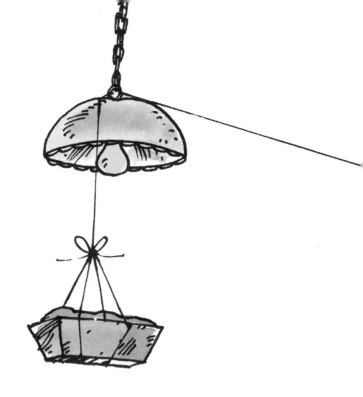

Amelia Bedelia got some string.

She worked for a bit.

And that bread began to rise.

"That should be high enough,"

said Amelia Bedelia.

"I'll just let you stay there awhile."

Amelia Bedelia picked up her list.

"Make a sponge cake."

Amelia Bedelia read that again.

"I know about a lot of cakes,"

she said.

"And I never heard of that.

But if she wants a sponge cake,

I'll make her a sponge cake."

Amelia Bedelia put a little of this
and some of that into a bowl.
She mixed and mixed.
"Now for the sponge," she said.
Amelia Bedelia got a sponge.
She snipped it into small pieces.
"There," she said.
"Into the cake you go."

Soon the sponge cake was baking.

"I don't think Mr. Rogers

will like this cake,"

said Amelia Bedelia.

"I'll make my kind of cake too.

He does love butterscotch icing."

So Amelia Bedelia

baked another cake.

"There now," she said.

"I'll surprise him."

Amelia Bedelia put

the butterscotch cake in the cupboard.

She put the sponge cake on a shelf.

"My, this is a busy day,"
said Amelia Bedelia.
"Let's see what's next.
'Call Alcolu. Ask him to patch
the front door screen.'"
Amelia Bedelia shook her head.
"Alcolu can't patch anything,"
she said. "I better do that myself."
She got what she needed.

And Amelia Bedelia patched that screen.

Amelia Bedelia looked at the time.

"Oh," she said.

"I better get dinner started.

Let me see what she wants."

She read the list.

"A chicken dinner will be fine."

Amelia Bedelia shook her head.

"What will she think of next?" she said.

"Well, that won't take long to fix."

Amelia Bedelia got everything ready.

She set the table.

Then she sat down to rest.

Soon Mr. and Mrs. Rogers came home.

"Amelia Bedelia," yelled Mr. Rogers.

"Coming," called Amelia Bedelia.

"What is that awful cloth

on the front door?" asked Mrs. Rogers.

"You said to patch the screen,"
said Amelia Bedelia.

"Can't patch without a patch."

They went into the parlor.

"All my good pots!" said Mrs. Rogers.

"And bad ones too,"

said Amelia Bedelia.

41

Mr. Rogers looked at the wood box.

He shook his head.

But he didn't say a word.

They went into the kitchen.

"The sponge cake is pretty,"

said Mrs. Rogers.

"At least that's done right."

Something caught Mr. Rogers's eye.

He looked up.

"What in tarnation is that?" he said.

"The bread!" said Amelia Bedelia.

"I plumb forgot it.

Do let me punch it down quick."

She climbed up on a chair.

Amelia Bedelia began to punch.

Mr. and Mrs. Rogers just stared.

The bread plopped to the floor.

"Did I see what I thought I saw?"
said Mr. Rogers.

"You did," said Mrs. Rogers.

"Now," said Amelia Bedelia,

"dinner is ready when you are."

"Well, you can cook," said Mrs. Rogers.

"Dinner should be good."

"I hope so," said Mr. Rogers.

"I'm hungry."

"Just serve the plates,"

said Mrs. Rogers.

Mr. and Mrs. Rogers sat at the table.

Amelia Bedelia brought in the plates.

Mr. and Mrs. Rogers stared at the plates.

"But, but, that's cracked corn.

It's all kinds of awful things,"

said Mrs. Rogers.

"You said chicken dinner,"

said Amelia Bedelia.

"That's what chickens eat for dinner."

Mrs. Rogers was too angry to speak.

"Take this mess away,"

said Mr. Rogers.

Mrs. Rogers said,

"Serve the cake and coffee."

Amelia Bedelia did.

Mr. Rogers took a big bite of cake.

He spluttered and spit it out.

"What in tarnation is in that?" he said.

"Sponge," said Amelia Bedelia.

"Mrs. Rogers said

to make a sponge cake."

Suddenly Mr. Rogers laughed.

He roared.

Mrs. Rogers looked at the lumpy cake.

Then she laughed too.

"But I'm still hungry,"

said Mr. Rogers.

"I can fix that," said Amelia Bedelia.

"I have a surprise for you."

"Oh, no!" said Mr. Rogers.

"I can't stand another one,"

said Mrs. Rogers.

Amelia Bedelia brought in milk

and her butterscotch cake.

"Ahh," said Mr. Rogers.

"Hurry," said Mrs. Rogers.

"Give me some."

Soon the whole cake was gone.

"How do you do it, Amelia Bedelia?"
said Mr. Rogers. "One minute
we're hopping mad at you."
"And the next, we know we can't
do without you," said Mrs. Rogers.

Amelia Bedelia smiled.

"I guess I just understand your ways," she said.

Read all the books about
Amelia Bedelia

Amelia Bedelia
by Peggy Parish
pictures by Fritz Siebel

Thank You, Amelia Bedelia
by Peggy Parish
pictures by Barbara Siebel Thomas

Amelia Bedelia and the Surprise Shower
by Peggy Parish
pictures by Barbara Siebel Thomas

Come Back, Amelia Bedelia
by Peggy Parish
pictures by Wallace Tripp

Play Ball, Amelia Bedelia
by Peggy Parish
pictures by Wallace Tripp

Teach Us, Amelia Bedelia
by Peggy Parish
pictures by Lynn Sweat

Good Work, Amelia Bedelia
by Peggy Parish
pictures by Lynn Sweat

Amelia Bedelia Helps Out
by Peggy Parish
pictures by Lynn Sweat

Amelia Bedelia and the Baby
by Peggy Parish
pictures by Lynn Sweat

Amelia Bedelia Goes Camping
by Peggy Parish
pictures by Lynn Sweat

Merry Christmas, Amelia Bedelia
by Peggy Parish
pictures by Lynn Sweat

Amelia Bedelia's Family Album
by Peggy Parish
pictures by Lynn Sweat

Good Driving, Amelia Bedelia
by Herman Parish
pictures by Lynn Sweat

Bravo, Amelia Bedelia!
by Herman Parish
pictures by Lynn Sweat

Amelia Bedelia 4 Mayor
by Herman Parish
pictures by Lynn Sweat

Calling Doctor Amelia Bedelia
by Herman Parish
pictures by Lynn Sweat

Amelia Bedelia, Bookworm
by Herman Parish
pictures by Lynn Sweat

Happy Haunting, Amelia Bedelia
by Herman Parish
pictures by Lynn Sweat

Amelia Bedelia, Rocket Scientist?
by Herman Parish
pictures by Lynn Sweat

Amelia Bedelia Under Construction
by Herman Parish
pictures by Lynn Sweat

Peggy Parish

first created Amelia Bedelia in 1963 and wrote a total of twelve books about the zany antics of this charming housekeeper. Amelia Bedelia is one of the most beloved children's book characters of all time.

Lynn Sweat

has illustrated many Amelia Bedelia books, including *Bravo, Amelia Bedelia!*; *Amelia Bedelia and the Baby*; and *Amelia Bedelia, Rocket Scientist?* He is a painter as well as an illustrator, and his paintings hang in galleries across the country. He and his wife live in Connecticut.